For Reto, for enduring all the noisy neighbors
(and sometimes being one) with me —K.E.

For my nieces, Karys, Peyton, Myla,
Jaylen, Ferrah, and Solei —A.F.

Text copyright © 2021 by Kristy Everington
Jacket art and interior illustrations copyright © 2021 by AG Ford

All rights reserved. Published in the United States by Random House Studio, an imprint of
Random House Children's Books, a division of Penguin Random House LLC, New York.

Random House Studio and the colophon are registered trademarks of Penguin Random House LLC.

Visit us on the Web! rhcbooks.com

Educators and librarians, for a variety of teaching tools, visit us at RHTeachersLibrarians.com

Library of Congress Cataloging-in-Publication Data is available upon request.
ISBN 978-0-593-17810-2 (trade) — ISBN 978-0-593-17811-9 (lib. bdg.) — ISBN 978-0-593-17812-6 (ebook)

MANUFACTURED IN CHINA
10 9 8 7 6 5 4 3 2 1
First Edition

Isobel
Adds It Up

By **Kristy Everington**

Illustrated by **AG Ford**

RANDOM HOUSE STUDIO

Isobel loved math.
She loved the soft curves of the number three,
the hard edge of seven,
and how numbers always made sense to her.
In the quiet of her room, she sharpened her pencil
and zipped through her homework.

And then the new neighbors moved in next door.

They made loud noises.
They bumped.
They clomped.
They banged.
They stomped.

Isobel said, "I think acrobats live next door."

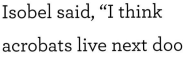

She couldn't concentrate with all the noise.

She had subtractions,

additions,

multiplications,
all due Monday.

She tried working in the garden,
but her subtractions got soaked in the rain.

Inside, the rumbles got louder.

The trumpets grew shrill.

The stomping shook the walls.

Isobel couldn't think!

She said, "I think a marching band lives next door."
She shushed them as loudly as she could,
but the trombone just growled for longer.

She stuck tissues in her ears and wedged herself in a cupboard,
but it was too dark to do addition.
And she could still hear the neighbors.
They danced and they shouted
and played their music loud.

She tried to count the drumbeats
but couldn't keep track of the numbers.
"That marching band has no manners!" Isobel cried.

She decided she would play her own music loud
and see how they liked that.

She turned the volume up as far as it would go.
Her music mixed with theirs—
what a ruckus!

Finally their music stopped . . .
but then Isobel heard the neighbors dancing
and singing to her song.

She stamped her feet up and down,

making nearly as much noise as the neighbors.

Isobel had never handed homework in late before.
She stared at her math problems,
but the sounds of party poppers and a
conga line made it impossible to focus.

Numbers didn't make sense to her anymore.

Not even tracing the curves of three could cheer her up.

She had to do something about the racket!

THUNK.
THUNK.
SWISH!

"There, did you hear that?" Isobel asked her father. "That's a ball bouncing on the floor! I think a basketball team lives next door."

Isobel had an idea.

She made peanut butter cookies

because she liked measuring flour with the ¾ cup,

and everyone knows peanut butter cookies are the best.

She left them on the neighbors'
doorstep with a note:

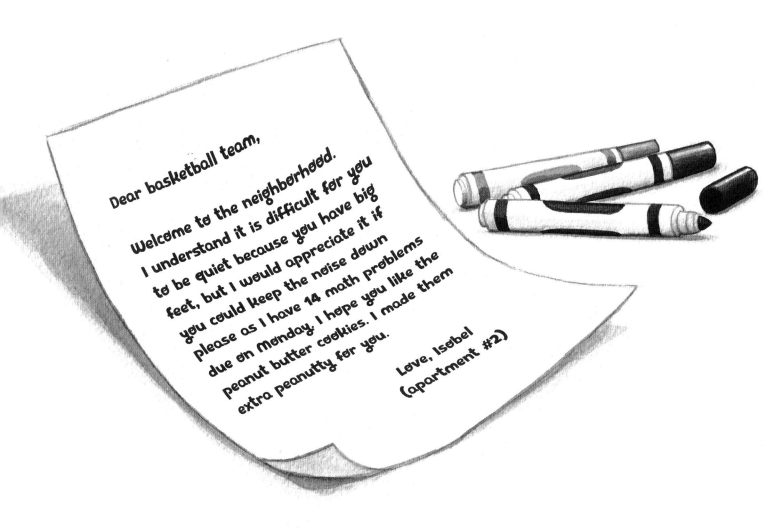

Dear basketball team,

Welcome to the neighborhood.
I understand it is difficult for you
to be quiet because you have big
feet, but I would appreciate it if
you could keep the noise down
please as I have 14 math problems
due on Monday. I hope you like the
peanut butter cookies. I made them
extra peanutty for you.

Love, Isobel
(apartment #2)

That evening, a note got slipped under her door.

TO ISOBEL,

SORRY ABOUT THE NOISE. THANKS FOR
BEING UNDERSTANDING—WE DO HAVE
BIG FEET. WE WILL TRY TO BE MORE QUIET.
THANKS FOR THE COOKIES! PEANUT
BUTTER IS MY FAVORITE. I ALSO
HAVE MATH HOMEWORK DUE ON
MONDAY—MAYBE WE COULD
STUDY TOGETHER?

LOVE FROM BERNADETTE
(NEXT DOOR)

Isobel wasn't sure.
She loved quiet, and Bernadette made
an awful lot of noise.

The next day, there was a loud knock.

Bernadette was not what Isobel imagined . . .

and it turned out she was an excellent study partner after all.

They could do subtractions outside even when it rained.

Bernadette was fantastic at times tables.
She could remember 6 × 7 every time—
after all, an elephant never forgets.

They baked different peanut treats together.

Isobel measured, and Bernadette cleaned up.

When it got too loud inside, Bernadette helped with that too.

They both finished their math problems on time. And sometimes . . .

Isobel joined the ruckus next door.